A 20th Century Fox Presentation

ANASTASIA

A Don Bluth / Gary Goldman Film

Classic Edition

Adapted from the movie by A. L. Singer
Illustrated by Bob DePew

HarperActive™
A *Division of* HarperCollins*Publishers*

A 20th Century Fox Presentation

ANASTASIA

Classic Edition

Chapter 1

"Long live the Czar!"
"Long live the Princess!"
"Long live the Romanovs, each and every one!"

All around the ballroom of the Winter Palace, the guests' joyous voices rang out. Princess Anastasia Romanov heard them all. Their jewels flashed like fireflies in the chandelier light. But their faces were a blur. In her father's arms, Anastasia soared across the floor. Her head was light and her feet were tired, but she didn't care.

"To three hundred more years!" another voice bellowed.

Oh, please, yes! thought Anastasia. This year was a glorious anniversary—the three hundredth of her family's rule over Russia. But things were not going well. The peasants were threatening a revolution. And the family advisor—Rasputin, the so-called mystic— had turned traitor. Nowadays, even the thought of greasy, baggy-eyed Rasputin gave Anastasia the shivers.

Thank goodness her father, Czar Nicholas II, had banished him from the palace.

Anastasia hugged her father tightly. Soon he would have to dance with her mother and her three older sisters.

Anastasia wanted to savor every graceful step.

Thump. Alexi rammed into her from behind and tripped onto the dance floor. "Owww!"

"Careful!" Anastasia scolded her younger brother.

Alexi sat up and stuck out his tongue.

"The next czar of Russia," Anastasia said with a giggle, "should take some dance lessons."

Czar Nicholas laughed aloud. As the orchestra played its final chords, he bowed to Anastasia.

As she curtsied, she noticed the crowd beginning to part. Through the middle walked a regally dressed, silver-haired woman—Dowager Empress Marie, mother of the Czar.

Anastasia practically flew across the room. Her grandmother lived in Paris, so each visit was a rare treat. "Grandmama!" she shouted, clutching the Empress's hand. "You will stay a long time, won't you?"

"Anastasia," Empress Marie said with a sad smile, "I must return after the ball, but this time I'm leaving something with you. Something to remember me by."

In her hand was a delicate, jeweled wooden box.

"Is it a jewelry box?" Anastasia asked excitedly.

Empress Marie held a gold key in the shape of a flower. It hung on a necklace. She inserted it in the box, and a

haunting melody began.

"It's our lullaby!" Anastasia exclaimed.

"You can play it at night before you go to sleep, and pretend it's me singing." Empress Marie held out the key.

"Read what this inscription says."

Anastasia squinted. "TOGETHER IN PARIS," she read.

"Really? Am I going to Paris? Oh, Grandmama!"

Anastasia flung her arms around the Empress, but her grandmother did not hug her back. Empress Marie's face had lost its color. She was staring toward the door.

A chill blew through the ballroom. A woman screamed. People were scurrying aside, making room for a bearded, dark-cloaked visitor. His long, stringy hair swung limply as he scanned the crowd.

From the high-vaulted ceiling, a bat swooped downward. It perched on the man's shoulder as he trained his icy blue eyes on Czar Nicholas.

"You think you can banish the great Rasputin?" bellowed the unwanted guest. "It is I who will destroy you, mark my words! You and your family will die within the fortnight. I will not rest until I see the end of the Romanov line forever!"

Rasputin held aloft a heavy reliquary, dangling from a long cord. It was a glass cylinder, filled with a glowing liquid that pulsed and bubbled.

Crrrrack!

Anastasia jumped back. A bolt of lightning shot upward from the reliquary, cutting the chain holding the chandelier. It crashed to the floor, plunging the ballroom into darkness.

Anastasia clung to her father. Until now, she had never believed that Rasputin was truly a magical being. Now she did. And she was scared.

The cries of shock were fading behind Rasputin. As he stalked across the palace grounds, his eyes were on the heavy iron gates.

From beyond those gates came a different set of cries—the angry protests of a revolutionary mob. Their faces were twisted with rage. Some waved rifles. Others held aloft bricks and rocks.

Rasputin smiled. They were out for blood. But they were locked out. There was a simple remedy for that.

Hidden in the shadows, he held up his reliquary. "Fulfill my curse," he murmured, "and seal our dark bargain."

A bolt of light burst from the reliquary. It surrounded the gate and shattered the lock.

With a roar that echoed off the palace walls, the protesters stormed the gate. The bricks and stones flew through the palace windows. A group of burly men began pulling down a statue of the Czar.

Rasputin watched calmly. His work was finished.

And so were the Romanovs.

Chapter 2

Crrrack! Crrrack!

Rifle shots. Dimitri huddled in the dark tunnel behind the royal bedrooms. All around he could hear breaking glass, bloodthirsty shouts. The mob was in the palace now, and he was not going to move. After all, if the peasants wanted to kill the royal family, they would kill the servants too!

"Anastasia! Come back! Come back!"

Dimitri's ears pricked up at the nearby voice. What was the Empress doing upstairs?

"My music box!" shouted Princess Anastasia, just beyond the wall.

Crrrack! Crrrack!

The mob swarmed down the hallway. They were trapped.

Dimitri opened the secret panel in the bedroom wall. "Come this way, out the servants' quarters!"

He darted into the room and pushed both of them into the passageway. Something fell out of Anastasia's hand onto the floor.

"My music box!" she cried.

The bedroom door swung open behind them. "Forget the box." Dimitri slammed the secret panel shut.

Now he was alone in the room. An enormous man stomped in, clutching a rifle. "Where are they, boy?" he roared.

"Th-th-they're not here," Dimitri stammered.

The man hit Dimitri with the rifle butt. Groaning, he fell to the floor. As the man rampaged around the room, Dimitri reached for the fallen music box and hid it beneath himself.

Outside the window, a small white bat watched. Taking note of Anastasia and her grandmother's escape, he flew away to his master, Rasputin.

Anastasia followed her grandmother across the lawn, through the streets, over a frozen river. "Grandmama!" she cried out, stumbling on the ice.

"Keep up with me, darling!" Empress Marie cried.

The icy wind bit into Anastasia's face as she hurried toward a stone bridge. Under it, the ice would be thinner. They had to be careful—

"Aha!" A deep-throated cry rang out.

Anastasia screamed. From high atop the bridge, Rasputin jumped down. He landed hard, breaking through the ice. As he sank he grabbed Anastasia's ankle.

"You'll never escape me, child!" he cried. "Never!"

"Let me go!" Anastasia kicked against the iron grip.

With a sharp crack, the ice broke again. Rasputin fell backward into the frigid water. "Bartok!" he yelled.

"Master!" came a squeaky voice.

A bat swooped down toward Rasputin. But the bearded man's eyes rolled back. He sank beneath the river's surface, leaving only the glowing reliquary. And soon that was gone, too—flying through the air in the jaws of the bat.

"Come, Anastasia!" Empress Marie urged.

Numb from the cold—and the shock of Rasputin's death—Anastasia stumbled along blindly.

When they arrived at the St. Petersburg train station, the platform was teeming with people. Everyone pressed toward the train, panicked, trying to escape the revolt.

"Anastasia, hurry!" Just ahead, Empress Marie was being pulled onto the train.

Anastasia ran after her. "Grandmama!"

"Take my hand!"

Anastasia reached for her grandmother's outstretched hand. She clasped it tightly.

But the train was picking up speed. And the crowd was jostling against Anastasia, throwing her off balance. Her fingers were slipping, slipping . . .

"Anastasia!"

Anastasia lurched downward.

Her grandmother's desperate scream was the last sound Anastasia heard before her head hit the platform.

Chapter 3

"Psssst! Over here!" shouted a man dressed in rags.

Across the crowded street, a gap-toothed woman held up a pair of pajamas. "Fell off a truck! Big bargain."

"New calendars for 1926!" came a nasal voice.

All around Dimitri, desperate cries rang out. The cries of St. Petersburg's black market. The cries of poor, struggling people trying to make illegal money—because the legal money was never enough. Dimitri ignored them and closed his worn-out shirt collar against the cold.

Dimitri was well known on the street. Over the last ten years, since the fall of the Romanovs, he'd become one of the city's craftiest con artists.

But Dimitri was tired of being poor. He was twenty years old, strong, handsome, and ambitious. He wanted to escape Russia and see the world.

And now he had a plan. A perfect plan. For years, rumors had floated around the city. Rumors that Princess Anastasia had escaped the revolution and was still alive.

That was nonsense, of course, Dimitri thought. The entire royal family, except for Empress Marie, had been caught and executed. But Empress Marie, who lived in Paris, had offered an enormous reward if the rumors about Anastasia were proven true.

And Dimitri was determined to collect that reward.

After all, in a country as big as Russia, *some* eighteen-year-old girl could be a perfect impostor.

It was just a matter of finding her.

From among the crowd stepped Dimitri's friend Vladimir. He was an older man, and a bit . . . well, tubby. He had once been a wealthy aristocrat. Dimitri remembered seeing him often in the royal palace, flirting with the Empress's cousin Sophie. Nowadays, though, he was like everyone else in Russia. His fine wool suit was patched together and worn out.

And, like Dimitri, he was dying to escape.

Both men fell into step on the cobblestone street. "Well, I got us a theater," Vladimir whispered.

"Now all we need is the girl," Dimitri said. "Just think, Vlad—if this works, no more forging papers, no more stolen goods. We'll have three tickets out of here. One for you, one for me, and one for Anastasia. Imagine what Empress Marie will pay!"

"We'll be rich!" Vladimir declared.

Dimitri grinned. "And we'll be out of here!"

On the outskirts of the city, not far from the coast of the Baltic Sea, was a crumbling, run-down orphanage. Since the revolution, its

population had grown. Now the shrieks of children rang out night and day. So did the angry shouts of the director, Comrade Phlegmenkof.

People often told Comrade Phlegmenkof she ran a tight ship. Behind her back, they said she *resembled* one.

Only one person in the orphanage was tougher and more stubborn than Comrade Phlegmenkof—a red-haired girl who had just turned eighteen. She was called Anya, but no one knew her real name. Anya had come to the orphanage ten years earlier with a head injury that had caused her to lose her memory. Name, address, family—all forgotten. Her only possession had been a chain necklace with a small gold key in the shape of a rose hanging from it. On the back an inscription read: TOGETHER IN PARIS.

Anya was fingering that necklace, gazing out the orphanage window, when Comrade Phlegmenkof approached.

"Anya, I got you a job in the fish factory!" the orphanage director announced with a satisfied grin. "See that path? You follow it until you get to the fork in the road, go left, and . . . Anya, are you listening?"

"Yes, *Comrade* Phlegmenkof," Anya said absently.

Comrade Phlegmenkof scowled. "You've been a thorn in my side since you were brought here, acting like the Queen of Sheba instead of the nameless no-account you are! And for the last ten years I've fed you, I've clothed you, I've kept a roof over your head—"

Anya had heard this speech before. From the word *Sheba* she began reciting along with the director.

"How is it," Comrade Phlegmenkof said through gritted teeth,

"you don't have a clue to who you were before you came here, but you can remember all that?"

Anya turned from the window. "I *do* have a clue!" she insisted, holding out the necklace.

Comrade Phlegmenkof angrily grabbed it and read the inscription: "TOGETHER IN PARIS." She burst out laughing. "So, you want to go to France to find your family, huh? Little Miss Anya, it's time to take your place in life. And be grateful, too!"

As Comrade Phlegmenkof waddled away, Anya stormed out of the orphanage.

"'Be grateful,'" Anya mimicked. "I *am* grateful! Grateful to get away!"

How dare Comrade Phlegmenkof make fun of her? How dare she mock the inscription? Anya knew it meant something. "Whoever gave me this necklace must have loved me," she said to herself. Someday she'd find out who that person was.

Before long, Anya arrived at the fork in the road. An old sign pointed to Fisherman's Village on the left and St. Petersburg on the right. "Go left, she said," Anya murmured, fingering the gold key. "I know what's to the left. I'll be Anya the Orphan forever. But if I go to the right, maybe I could find a way to—" She shook her head. "This is crazy. Me, go to Paris?"

Anya looked up at the sky and closed her eyes. She prayed for a sign. A hint, a signal, *anything*!

Suddenly Anya gagged. Someone had grabbed her scarf. Her eyes sprang open and she saw her attacker—a flop-eared little dog.

"I don't have time to play right now!" she insisted. I'm waiting for—"

The dog yanked hard and Anya fell into the snow. Barking madly, the dog was trying to pull her toward St. Petersburg.

A sign. Anya smiled. This was it!

"Okay," she said, standing up. "I can take a hint." Barking happily, the dog followed her down the path to the right.

The walk into St. Petersburg was long and tiring. But it was nothing compared to what she faced in the city. St. Petersburg was a city of lines—lines for bread, lines for milk, lines for paper. When you finished with one line, you went on to another.

By the time Anya reached the front of the travel-ticket line, she'd become best friends with her little dog. She even chose a name for him: Pooka.

Now, after what seemed like hours, Anya stepped up to a clerk. "One ticket to Paris, please."

The clerk glared at her. "Exit visa?"

"Exit visa?" Anya repeated.

"No exit visa, no ticket!" The clerk slapped a sign onto his window that read PEOPLE'S LUNCH BREAK, then slammed the shutters in Anya's face.

Tears welled up in her eyes. Pooka began nuzzling against her.

"Psssst!" a voice hissed.

Anya turned to see an old sweeper woman. She was walking

toward Anya, leaving her pile of leaves at the curb. "See Dimitri," she whispered. "He can help you."

"Where can I find him?" Anya asked timidly.

"At the old palace," the old woman replied, pointing beyond the town square. "But you didn't hear it from me!"

Dimitri. Anya locked the name in her mind. "Thank you," she whispered.

Wiping her tears, she set off for the old Winter Palace.

Chapter 4

"We're doomed!" Dimitri moaned to Vladimir.

The two men walked briskly away from the St. Petersburg Art Theater. The audition had been horrible. Not one girl had come close to being a believable Anastasia. *Girl?* Some of them looked as old as Empress Marie!

Vladimir nodded sadly. "That's it. Game over."

"She's *got* to be here somewhere, Vlad, right under our noses!" Reaching into his backpack, Dimitri pulled out a jeweled box—the old music box he had taken from the palace so many years ago. "One look at this and the Empress will think we've brought the real Anastasia. Before she catches on, we'll be off spending the ten million rubles!"

Hope. Hope. Hope.

It was the only thing keeping their spirits up as they walked toward the old Winter Palace. The two friends lived there, hidden among the secret passageways Dimitri had memorized as a child. The palace was not at all the way it used to be. Nowadays it was abandoned and drafty and dark.

But it was still the biggest house in town.

The afternoon sunlight slanted across the Winter Palace dome, casting long shadows. Anya was not impressed. No guards, no flags, not even a decent lawn. Just a big old hulk, the size of a small city but in need of a paint job.

Anya slowly approached the front entrance. The door was gone, but boards had been nailed across it.

Pooka scurried through a small space at the bottom.

"Pooka!" Anya cried out. She pulled on the old wooden boards. One of them came loose and fell to the floor.

Anya stepped into the darkness. Her footsteps clattered on the marble floor. Around her, dusty shafts of light angled into a grand parlor through holes in the wall. Thick dust coated bulky furniture. On the walls were dark portrait paintings. Nothing had been covered up. *Someone must have left in an awful hurry*, Anya thought.

"Hello?" Anya called out. "Anybody home?"

No answer. She moved onward, to the top of a grand, carpeted staircase. There, in a vestibule, hung a portrait of a royal family. A bearded czar with kind eyes. A lovely czarina. Four young daughters and a little son. They were somehow familiar. Especially the youngest daughter. Anya smiled when she realized why—the girl looked like a younger version of herself!

Anya turned away and found herself at the top of a grand staircase. Below her was the most magnificent space she had ever

seen—a grand ballroom that could fit the entire orphanage and then some!

She flew down the stairs. Her feet guided her across the floor—*one*-two-three, *one*-two-three—dancing!

How do I know how to do this?

The words shot through her mind, but they gave way to a glorious daydream. In it, the kind-looking czar was stepping out of the painting, taking her hand—

"Hey! What are you doing in here?"

Anya jumped in surprise. The dream vanished like smoke from a blown-out match. Across the ballroom, two men ran toward her—one young and dark-haired, the other plump and balding.

Anya ran back up the stairs. The younger man sprinted up behind her, scooping up Pooka and grabbing Anya's arm, just under the portrait.

"How did you get in here?" he demanded. But his eyes were darting upward, toward the portrait. "Vlad!" he whispered over his shoulder. "Do you see what I see?"

"Oh, yes, yes . . ." the older man agreed.

"Are you Dimitri?" Anya asked.

The young man raised a suspicious eyebrow and handed Pooka to Vladimir. "That depends on who's looking for him."

"My name's Anya. I need travel papers. They say you're the man to see. . . ."

Dimitri was circling around her now, still eyeing the portrait.

"You know, you look an awful lot like . . . never mind! Now, you said something about travel papers?"

"Yes," Anya replied. "I'd like to go to Paris."

"Paris?" Dimitri grinned and cast Vladimir a look.

But Vladimir didn't pay attention. Pooka was licking his face. "Oh, oh!" he said with a giggle. "He likes me!"

Dimitri spun back around. "Anya . . . is there a last name that goes with that?"

"Well, this is going to sound crazy," Anya answered, "but I don't know my last name. I was found wandering around when I was eight years old. I don't remember anything before that. But I do have one clue: Paris. So can you two help me or not?"

Dimitri whispered something to Vladimir, who instantly pulled three tickets out of his coat pocket.

"Oddly enough," Dimitri said, "we're going to Paris ourselves. Uh, I've got three tickets right here. Unfortunately, the third one is for Anastasia."

Anya tried to read the tickets, but Vladimir pulled them away. "Anastasia who?" she asked.

"Romanov," Dimitri answered, gesturing toward one of the portraits on the wall. This one showed the youngest daughter, hand in hand with a regal-looking older woman.

"We're going to reunite the Grand Duchess Anastasia with her grandmother," Vladimir explained.

"You know, you do kind of resemble her," Dimitri remarked.

"The same age, the same physical type. Those blue Romanov eyes, Alexandra's chin . . ."

"Nicholas's smile," Vladimir added, taking Anya's hand. "Look, she even has the grandmother's hands!"

Anya yanked her hand away. "Are you trying to tell me you think I'm Anastasia?"

"I have seen thousands of girls all over the country," Dimitri explained, "and not one of them looks as much like the Grand Duchess as you do!"

"I think you are both crazy!" Anya declared, turning to leave.

"Why?" Dimitri pleaded. "You don't remember what happened to you . . . you're looking for family in Paris."

"No one knows what happened to *her*," Vladimir added, "and her only family is in Paris. . . ."

"Ever thought of the possibility?" Dimitri asked.

Anya stopped and faced the two men. The vision of the ballroom flashed through her mind again—the colors, the lights, the joy that felt so distantly familiar. "It's hard to think of yourself as a duchess when you're sleeping on a damp floor. But, sure . . . yeah. I guess *every* lonely girl would hope she's a princess."

"And somewhere, one girl *is*," Vladimir said. "After all, the name Anastasia means 'She will rise again.'"

"Well, wish we could help," Dimitri said, taking Vladimir's arm, "but the third ticket is for Grand Duchess Anastasia. Good luck."

As the two men walked away, Anya felt a tug in her heart. She gazed up at the portrait of Princess Anastasia and the Empress.

Could it be? No way. It made no sense. Still . . .

"Dimitri, wait!" Anya ran down the stairs and caught up to the men. "If I'm not Anastasia, the Empress will know right away, and it's just an honest mistake, right?"

Vladimir nodded. "But if you *are* the Princess, then you'll finally know who you are and have your family back."

"Either way, it gets you to Paris!" Dimitri exclaimed.

Anya took a deep breath. It was now or never. "Right!" she said, extending her hand.

Dimitri looked shocked. A smile spread across his face and he took her hand.

Anya squeezed firmly.

"Owww!" Dimitri cried out.

Anya giggled. He was cute, but he had a weak handshake.

And he was her ticket to a new life.

Chapter 5

"May I present Her Royal Highness," Dimitri shouted into the ballroom, *"Grand Duchess Anastasia!"*

The name echoed upward, to the rafters. There, a sleeping bat opened his eyes. "Anastasia?" repeated Bartok.

Behind him hung the reliquary of Rasputin, covered with dust and cobwebs. It began to glow.

Bartok screamed. The glow could mean only one thing—the Romanov curse had not been fulfilled. "It can't be! The Romanovs are all dead!"

He gazed down at the ballroom. At the two laughing men and the young, red-haired woman between them.

"It is she!" Bartok said with a gasp. "Anastasia!"

The reliquary suddenly shot through the air. Its cord wrapped around Bartok's foot.

Shrieking with fear, Bartok was pulled through a hole in the roof. Suddenly he was rocketing across the frozen city—and then plunging into the Neva River!

The reliquary struck the murky bottom and kept going,

burrowing through the earth itself.

Thwomp! Bartok dropped into a cavern and landed on a rock floor. He tried to hop to his feet. But a cold, bony hand closed around his chest.

"Who dares intrude on my solitude?" thundered the long-forgotten voice of Rasputin. "Get out!"

"Master!" Bartok squeaked. "You're alive!"

"In a manner of speaking." Rasputin—or some ghostly form of him—opened his hand. As Bartok fell to the ground, one of the old magician's eyeballs popped out.

Bartok quickly handed it back.

"Something's happened, hasn't it?" Rasputin growled, calmly replacing the eye. "I could feel the dark forces stirring. What is it, Bartok? Tell me!"

"I saw her, sir," Bartok replied. "Anastasia!"

Rasputin's face reddened. "Anastasia? Alive? So *that's* why I'm here in limbo!" With a yowl of rage, he gripped Bartok and punched his fist into the air.

Zzzzing! The fist disconnected from his wrist. It thudded against the wall and dropped, still holding Bartok.

Bartok scrambled to his feet, dragging the hand back.

"Look at me!" Rasputin collapsed on a stone bed. "I'm falling apart! I'm a wreck!"

"Actually," Bartok said, "considering how long you've been dead, you look pretty good."

"If only I hadn't lost the key to my powers!"

"You mean this?" Bartok held up the reliquary.

"Where did you get that?" Rasputin sat up and grabbed the glowing cylinder. Laughing loudly, he held it high. "My destiny unfolds! Show me the little Romanov, and I swear, this time I will not fail!"

Bartok's breath caught in his throat. Creatures were emerging from the reliquary—slimy, winged beasts that flew around the room in a haze of glowing green.

"Minions!" Rasputin bellowed. *"Rise for your master!"*

With a grunt, Dimitri lifted his luggage onto the overhead rack of the train compartment. On the seat beside him, Vladimir was hunched over some onionskin paper, sl-o-o-owly writing with a quill pen.

By now, Vladimir was supposed to have forged travel papers for himself, Dimitri, and Anya. But here they were, already on the train to France, and Vladimir was still at it!

Dimitri plopped down across from Vladimir. Anya was on the seat next to him, nervously fingering her necklace.

"Stop fiddling with that thing," Dimitri said. "And sit up straight. Remember, you're a grand duchess!"

"How is it you know what grand duchesses do or don't do?" Anya demanded.

"I make it my business to know," Dimitri replied.

"Well, if you think I'm royalty, then stop bossing me around!" Anya stood up and left the passenger compartment.

"Well," Vladimir said with a chuckle. "She certainly has a mind of her own."

Dimitri's sour mood was only getting worse. With a sigh, Dimitri followed Anya to another compartment. This one was empty, and he sat across from her. "Look, I think we got off on the wrong foot."

"I think we did too," Anya replied. "But I do appreciate your apology."

"Who said anything about an apology?" Dimitri retorted.

Anya rolled her eyes. "Please don't talk anymore. It's only going to upset me."

"Fine!" Dimitri snapped.

Anya stared out the window at the snow-covered countryside. "Dimitri, do you think you'll miss Russia?"

"Nope."

"But it was your home."

"It was a place I once lived in. End of story."

"Then you must plan on making Paris your true home."

"What is it with you and *homes*?"

Anya rose angrily. "Well, for one thing, it's something every normal person wants, and for another—"

As Dimitri stood up to face her, Vladimir walked into the compartment, holding Pooka.

"Please remove Dimitri from my sight!" Anya commanded Vladimir.

Vladimir gave Dimitri a look. "What have you done to her?"

"Me?" Dimitri sputtered. "It's her!"

"Ha!" Anya spun away, left the compartment, and slammed the door behind her.

Vladimir smiled slyly. "An unspoken attraction?"

"*Attraction,* to that skinny brat? Have you lost your mind?" Dimitri bolted into the corridor.

Dimitri and Anya did not speak the rest of the day. That night, Dimitri could not sleep. As Anya dozed in the seat opposite him, he stared listlessly out the window. Every few moments he heard Vladimir's and Pooka's footsteps, pacing the train corridor.

When Vladimir finally entered the compartment, his face was pale. "It's what I hate about this government—everything's in red! I just overheard that all traveling papers must be in red ink!" Vladimir held out his forged papers, neatly written in black. "I propose we move to the baggage car—quickly, before the guards come!"

Dimitri flew into action. He pulled his baggage down from the rack. "Hey!" he yelled, nudging Anya.

Her eyes flickered. Her fist flew out and connected with Dimitri's nose.

"Owww!" Dimitri fell backward into the opposite seat.

Anya bolted upright. "Sorry, I thought you were some—oh, it's you, Dimitri. Well, that's okay, then."

Dimitri ignored the comment. He could hear the ticket collector approaching. Vladimir was already in the corridor, loaded down with luggage. Wincing, Dimitri pulled Anya out of the compartment. "Come on, we have to go!"

"Where are we going?" Anya demanded.

"I think you broke my nose!" Dimitri cried. Anya yanked her coat from the seat. "Men are such babies," she murmured.

In the confusion, no one noticed Pooka. He was growling and barking out the window—at the ugly green creatures that were flying by, on their way to the engine.

Anya shivered as she followed Dimitri into a cramped, unheated car. "The baggage car?" she asked, raising a sarcastic eyebrow. "There wouldn't be anything wrong with our papers, would there, *maestro*?"

"Of course not, *Your Grace*," Dimitri shot back. "I just hate to see you forced to mingle with all those commoners."

KAAA-BOOOOM!

The train jolted. Anya, Dimitri, Vladimir, and Pooka went flying. They landed in a heap of spilled suitcases.

"What was that?" Dimitri exclaimed.

Out the rear window, the rest of the train was pulling away, slowing down. The coupling was broken.

Vladimir ran to the front window. Just ahead of them was the locomotive, still attached—and going so fast that the engine was in

flames! "Uh, Dimitri," Vladimir said, "I think someone has flambéed our engine."

"Something's not right," Dimitri muttered. "Wait here, I'll check it out."

Dimitri pushed his way through the baggage-car door. The heat from the engine hit him like a blast furnace. Shielding his eyes, he climbed into the engineer's cockpit.

The seat was empty. The train was out of control.

Dimitri jumped into the seat. On the dashboard, the pressure gauges were all deep into the danger area. He grabbed a lever that looked like a brake.

Tssssss! It sizzled as it touched his skin.

"Yeeeeow!" Dimitri cried.

KA-BAMMMM! Flames burst from the dashboard. *Green* flames. Dimitri had never seen anything like them.

He scrambled back to the baggage car. "Nobody's driving this train! We're going to have to jump!"

He, Vladimir, and Anya ran to the side window.

The track dropped off to a sheer cliff. Way below, obscured by clouds, a river wandered.

Dimitri felt sick just looking at it.

"After you," Anya said.

Chapter 6

Floating below the baggage car, Rasputin's minions grinned wickedly. Their job was almost done.

They were prepared to fly away, when Dimitri's voice shouted from above: "I know! We'll uncouple the car!"

That was what he thought.

Quickly the minions set to work. With a flash of electric heat, they welded the coupling together. The baggage car was permanently connected to the engine.

Only one more step. One more step, and the death of the Princess would be assured.

A mile ahead of them was a high trestle bridge.

Perfect location.

Cackling, the minions flew toward it.

Dimitri pulled open the door that led to the engine. Below him the tracks were a blur. Standing on the ledge between cars, he tried to yank the coupling free. It would not budge. "I need a wrench, an axe, *anything*!" he yelled.

Vladimir raced toward a toolbox in the corner. But Anya's eyes were on Pooka. He was wagging his tail, barking at a wooden crate.

A crate labeled EXPLOSIVES, near a box of matches.

Anya pulled open the crate. She ran to Dimitri with a lit stick of dynamite.

Dimitri smiled. "That'll work." He jammed the stick into the coupling and jumped back into the baggage car.

He, Vladimir, Anya, and Pooka raced to the other end of the car and dived behind a steamer trunk. "What do they teach you in those orphanages?" Dimitri muttered.

The front of the car blasted apart in a shower of splinters and mangled metal. Now the engine was by itself, racing away from them toward a distant trestle bridge.

"Don't worry," Dimitri said. "We've got plenty of track. We'll just coast to a stop."

BROOOOOMMMMMMMMM!

The explosion ahead was so bright, Dimitri had to shield his eyes. And when it was over, the trestle bridge was crumbling into the water like a pile of sticks.

"You were saying?" Anya asked.

Dimitri thought fast. There had to be a way to brake this car. He would have to secure the axle to something.

Which meant going under the train.

On the floor was a chain with a grappling hook. Dimitri grabbed it and handed it to Vladimir. Then he ran to the

blast-scarred edge of the car and looked over.

The tracks whizzed by. Swallowing hard, he lowered himself carefully under the car, locking his hands and feet on metal braces. *"Hand me the chain!"* he cried.

Shaking with fright, Vladimir fell into a box. Anya grabbed the chain and ran it to the edge of the car.

Leaning over, she handed it to Dimitri.

"Not you!" Dimitri shouted.

"Vlad's busy at the moment," Anya replied.

Dimitri wrapped one end of the chain around the axle.

Just then, with a loud *crunch,* a chunk of loose metal fell from the car onto the track.

"Aaaaaaggggghhh!" screamed Dimitri.

Anya clutched his arm. As she pulled him up, the metal bounced off the track and sliced a nearby tree in two.

Dimitri's heart pounded as he held Anya. His eyes met hers. And lingered. Just for a moment.

Anya pulled away first. "Just think, that tree could have been you."

"If we live through this," Dimitri grumbled, "remind me to thank you."

This was no time for small talk. Ahead of them, the bridge gave way to a deep gorge. Dimitri took a deep breath and swung the chain like a lasso. If he could only hook a railroad tie . . .

"Here goes nothing," he said. "Brace yourselves."

With a grunt, he tossed the hook.

It bounced off the track bed with a loud *thunk,* twisting high in the air like an injured bird. Then it plunged back to the track—and snagged a railroad tie.

Dimitri opened his mouth to cheer.

But the tie ripped out of the ground like a matchstick.

The car didn't slow a bit.

And Dimitri's cheer became a silent scream.

Chapter 7

Snap! Snap! Snap!

One railroad tie after the other, pulling right out of the ground. Rasputin howled with laughter at the image in his reliquary. The Princess was doomed.

GRRRRONK!

The noise silenced him. His eyes almost popped out.

The sixth tie had caught. The chain was taut. The carriage of the car ripped right off its chassis. It crashed into the soft snowbank along the road.

As the engine plunged into the gorge, the Princess and her pals jumped out of the car. *Alive!*

Rasputin dropped the reliquary. *"Noooooooo! How could they let her escape?"*

"Now, take it easy there, you really should watch your blood pressure," said Bartok. He picked up the reliquary, which was now dark. "Guess this is broken," he remarked, tossing the reliquary over his shoulder.

"You idiot!" In terror, Rasputin flung out his arm. His hand

kept going. It flew under the reliquary and caught it. "I sold a piece of myself to harness this power! To destroy the Romanovs! If this reliquary breaks and these demons escape, they'll come for the rest of me—and maybe you too! Meddling rodent!"

"Oh, sure, blame the bat . . ." Bartok mumbled. "What the heck? We're easy targets, just hanging around. . . ."

Rasputin ignored him. He paced the lair, his gray face lined with fury. "I need something *really* fiendish!"

Vladimir danced through the Latvian countryside, picking crocuses out of the melting snow. He skipped ahead of Anya and Dimitri, with Pooka yipping at his heels.

"Sophie, my dear," he sang out, "Vlady's on his way!"

"Who's Sophie?" Anya asked.

"She is a tender little morsel! She is the cup of hot chocolate after a long walk in the snow!" Vladimir replied. "The Empress's ravishing first cousin."

"Nobody gets near the Dowager Empress without convincing Sophie first," Dimitri explained.

Anya shook her head in dismay. "Ohhh, no, not me! Nobody ever told me I had to *prove* I was the Grand Duchess. Show up, yes. Look nice, fine. But *lie*?"

"You don't know it's a lie," Dimitri insisted.

"Look at me, Dimitri!" Anya pleaded. "I'm not exactly grand duchess material!"

In a huff, she walked ahead to a small bridge. There, Vladimir was gazing dreamily into the water. He smiled at Anya. "Tell me, child . . . what do you see?"

Anya looked down at the water's smooth surface. What an awful reflection! A smudge-faced street urchin, dressed in raggedy boy's clothing. "I see a skinny little nobody, with no past and no future."

"I see an engaging and fiery young woman," Vladimir countered, "who on a number of occasions has shown a regal command equal to any royalty in the world. And I have known my share of royalty."

Anya was soothed by the words. The plan was insane, no doubt about it—but what was the alternative? Living in Comrade Phlegmenkof's orphanage?

"There's nothing left for you back there, my dear," Vladimir said softly. "Everything is in Paris."

By now, Dimitri was standing beside her. Anya had to fight back a sneer. But she was already making up her mind.

"Gentlemen," she said, "start your teaching."

Chapter 8

Anya adjusted the shoulder of the silk dress. She stepped carefully down toward the deck of the cargo ship.

For an obnoxious guy, Dimitri was full of mystery. How had he managed to get himself, Anya, Vladimir, and Pooka aboard the ship? How had he been able to buy the dress?

Anya had no idea. All she knew was that she was heading toward France across the Baltic Sea—in a silk gown that made her feel regal.

Vladimir and Dimitri were staring at her, frozen in the middle of a chess game. "Marvelous!" Vladimir cried out. "And now that you're dressed for a ball, you will learn to dance at one!"

Anya stepped onto the deck and held out her arms. Dimitri stood up awkwardly and joined her. "I'm not very good. . . ."

"And a *one*-two-three, *one*-two-three . . ." Vladimir counted out. "Anya, let *him* lead!"

Anya felt clumsy at first. But somehow, the steps came to her. She and Dimitri glided across the deck.

"That dress is really beautiful," Dimitri said gently.

Anya's face brightened. "Do you think so?"

A compliment! A real, live compliment from the con man of Russia! And he was smiling, too. A smile full of warmth and honesty.

Anya grinned. She felt giddy, light-headed. The sun was setting spectacularly on the sea, but all she saw were Dimitri's eyes. "I'm feeling a little dizzy."

"Me too," Dimitri said, his lips moving closer to hers. "Anya, I . . ."

"Yes?" Anya asked.

Rowf! Rowf!

Pooka's bark broke the spell. Dimitri backed off with a start. "You're . . . uh, doing fine."

He wandered away, his knees shaking.

Anya felt like a balloon that was quickly losing air.

That night, a storm hit the ship. Belowdecks, in a small, crowded cabin, Anya and Vladimir pitched back and forth with the rolling ship. Curled on the floor, Dimitri snored peacefully.

"Look at him!" Vladimir muttered. "He can sleep through anything."

The ship groaned, tilting suddenly upward. As Anya grabbed onto a handle, Pooka leaped into Dimitri's backpack.

Out tumbled a small jeweled box.

Anya's breath caught in her throat. It was as if an old dream had sprung from a dark corner of her mind.

"Pretty jewelry box, isn't it?" Vladimir remarked.

"Are you sure that's what it is?" Anya asked.

"What else could it be?"

"Something else. . . ." Anya struggled for words. "Something to do with a secret. Is that possible?"

Vladimir chuckled as he climbed into his bunk. "Anything's possible. You taught Dimitri how to waltz, didn't you? Sleep well, Your Majesty."

Anya settled into her bed, snuggling with Pooka. The storm was finally calming down, and so was she. Maybe the secret would come to her in a dream.

Deep underground, Rasputin was watching Anya closely in his reliquary. "Pleasant dreams to you, Princess," he hissed. "I'll get inside your mind, where you can't escape me!"

Out of the reliquary flew a wisp of a smoke. It shimmered with images, like the reflection in a river: trees, a field of grass, a happy family.

The smoke raced upward through the ground. It flew over the water, and into Anya's cabin. As she slept, the images entered her dreams.

Anya smiled. She saw herself in a vast meadow. A little boy surrounded by butterflies was waving at her.

Anya arose. Quietly she walked past the sleeping figures of Vladimir and Dimitri, then out into the corridor.

She let the door shut behind her and followed the butterflies up

to the deck. She was not aware of Pooka's yelping, nor his desperate scratching on the cabin door.

The little boy was beckoning Anya. To her, the ship's stairs were a rock embankment. The wet, rocking deck was a field of daffodils. As the rough seas tossed the ship, she staggered to the railing.

Overboard she saw a bright, peaceful pool. In it, three ecstatic girls were smiling at her. Anya wanted to join them. The desire overwhelmed her. She climbed over the railing.

Now she was standing on the narrow ledge that surrounded the ship. She tried to yell to the girls, but no sound came out. *I'm coming!* she thought. *I'm coming to you at last!*

There was only one way to do it. She bent her knees and prepared to dive into the raging black sea.

Chapter 9

"What, Pooka?" Dimitri groaned. He pushed away the little dog's face, but Pooka kept whining and nudging him.

Yawning, Dimitri sat up. Immediately he spotted Anya's empty bunk.

"Anya?" he called out.

No answer.

He ran out the door. Taking the steps two at a time, he climbed toward the deck.

As he emerged, his eyes fixed on the silhouette on the outside of the railing, soaked to the bone and barely hanging on.

His heart skipped a beat. *"Anyaaaaaa!"* he roared.

He raced toward her. The ship pitched violently. Dimitri's knees buckled.

As he struggled to stay upright, a wave washed overboard. It swept underneath him, lifting him upward . . . upward . . . toward the main mast. . . .

Dimitri grabbed a rope around the mast. As the wave dropped away, he held on and leaped into the crow's nest.

Below him, Anya was getting ready to jump.

"*Anya, no-o-o-o-o!*" Gripping the rope with both hands, Dimitri swung downward.

Anya stopped. She heard Dimitri, but another voice was shouting. This one was deep and angry. "*Jump!*" it commanded. "*The Romanov curse!*" Anya could see the face of a bearded madman, surrounded by ugly green creatures. Where was the boy she had followed?

Then Dimitri's arm was around her waist, pulling her back onto the deck. She whirled around to him, throwing her arms around his shoulders. "The Romanov curse . . ."

"What are you talking about?" Dimitri asked.

"I keep seeing faces!" Anya said, bursting into tears.

Dimitri held her close. "It was a nightmare. It's all right now. You're safe."

Rasputin dug his fingers into his face. Anastasia had been so close to death—so close! "*N-o-o-o!*" he shrieked.

"Easy, now, master," Bartok urged. "This is no time to lose your head."

"I'll have to kill her myself!" Rasputin declared.

"But that means going topside!" Bartok said. "You're *dead*, master. You're falling apart! Sir, excuse me, how do you expect to get to Paris in one piece?"

With a sinister grin, Rasputin raised his reliquary high. "I thought we'd take the train."

Cackling at the top of his lungs, Rasputin rocketed upward through the dirt ceiling.

chapter 10

"And where does Uncle Boris come from?" Dimitri whispered urgently. "Come on, you *know* this!"

Anya stood at the door of Empress Marie's mansion. As Dimitri quizzed her, Vladimir rang the bell. Facts about Anastasia and the Romanovs were now a big jumble in Anya's mind. Her knees were shaking. "What if Sophie doesn't recognize me?"

"She will!" Dimitri snapped. "You're Anastasia! Now, how does Anastasia like her tea?"

"With sugar and milk?" Anya tried.

Dimitri slapped his forehead with frustration. "No! You don't drink tea! Just hot water and lemon!"

The door opened, revealing a cheerful, heavyset woman who held a kitten. *"Oui, monsieur?"* she said.

"Sophie Stanislovskievna Somorkov-Smirnoff!" Vladimir cried.

Sophie beamed. "Vladimir Vanya Voinitsky Vasilovich! Well, this is unexpected. Come in!"

Sophie urged the three of them inside. The door slammed behind her in Pooka's face.

Vladimir gestured grandly to Anya. "May I present her Imperial

Highness, Grand Duchess Anastasia Nikolayevna!"

Sophie gasped. "Oh, my heavens, she certainly does look like Anastasia!" With a sad sigh, she looked at her kitten. "But so did many of the others, right, Tilly? Empress Marie has seen so many impostors lately."

Anya's hope was flying out the window.

Sophie led them all into a grand, carpeted parlor. Anya tried to stand straight, carrying herself like a princess. That was not too difficult.

Neither were most of Sophie's questions. Anya remembered everything Dimitri had told her.

With each answer, Sophie seemed more and more impressed. Finally, she took a deep breath and asked, "You'll most likely find this an impertinent question, but indulge me: How did you escape during the siege of the palace?"

Dimitri and Vladimir exchanged a nervous glance. Anya hadn't been told the answer to this.

But an image was taking shape in Anya's mind. An image locked up in her memory. "There was a boy," she said softly, "a boy who worked in the palace. He opened the wall. . . ." Suddenly she felt embarrassed. "I'm sorry. That sounds crazy."

Dimitri's face had lost its color. He stared at Anya, white as a sheet. Then, quietly, he left the room.

"So," Vladimir asked Sophie, "is she a Romanov?"

"Well," Sophie replied, "she answered every question."

Vladimir practically jumped out of his seat with glee. "So when do we go and see the Empress?"

"I'm afraid the Empress simply won't allow it," Sophie said. "But the Russian ballet is performing in Paris tonight—and the Dowager Empress and I *never* miss it."

Sophie gave Vladimir a meaningful look.

A smile spread across his face. He got the hint.

Outside, Dimitri was pacing around the garden, his mind in a fog. How could Anya have known about the wall? Only three people did. Two of them were alive, Empress Marie and Dimitri. The third, Anastasia, was dead. Or was she?

Vladimir scampered out of the house, his portly frame rocking from side to side. "We did it!" he crowed. "We're going to see the Imperial Highness tonight and get the ten million rubles—"

"Vlad," Dimitri interrupted, "she *is* the Princess."

Vladimir nodded. "Yes, Anya was extraordinary. I almost believed her!"

Now Anya was running into the garden. "Sophie wants to take us shopping for the ballet!" she shouted happily.

The accent. The brightness of her eyes. The tilt of her head as she smiled. It was all flooding back into Dimitri's mind. How could he not have seen it before?

He was sure now. Anya was Anastasia. In his great con game, he had conned only one person.

Himself.

Not far away, a train pulled into the Paris station. The passengers departed much more quickly than usual, for among them was a man of exceedingly foul appearance and putrid smell. A man with a pet bat and an unmistakable look of evil in his eyes.

Chapter 11

Dimitri and Vladimir paced the steps of the Paris Opera House, dressed in tuxedos. During their shopping trip with Sophie in Paris, Dimitri had not been able to confide the truth. Now, waiting for Anya's arrival, he let it pour out. "*I* was the boy in the palace, Vlad. The one who opened the wall. She's the real thing!"

Vladimir stopped in his tracks. His jaw dropped. "That means our Anya has found her family! We have found the heir to the Russian throne! And you . . ."

His voice wandered off. Dimitri tried to hide his tormented expression, but Vladimir's eyes were full of understanding. Vladimir knew that Dimitri had fallen in love.

"And I," Dimitri said, "will walk out of her life forever."

"But—you've got to tell her!" Vladimir insisted.

"Tell me what?" asked Anya.

Dimitri turned. Anya was climbing the steps. The most gifted artist in Paris could not have captured her radiance. The greatest poet could not describe what Dimitri felt.

"How beautiful you look," Dimitri answered Anya.

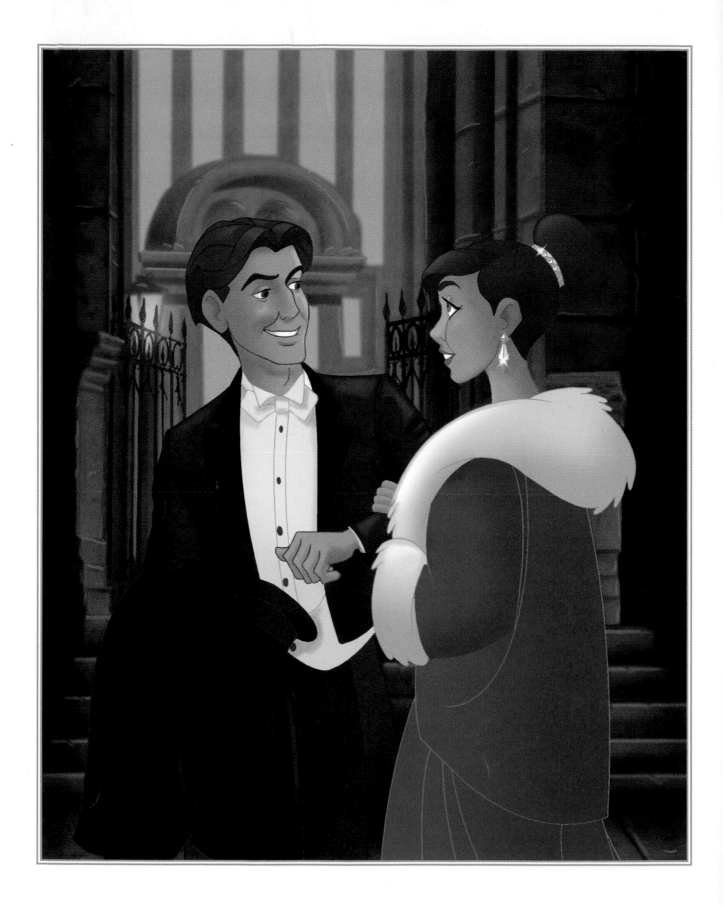

He offered his arm. She smiled and took it, and together they walked into the opera house.

Anya was surprised to see the intermission lights. She had not seen much of the ballet at all. During the entire first act, her heart had been thumping wildly. She'd been staring across the crowded theater at the box seats. At the elegant woman she was supposed to convince.

As the opera goers began filing into the aisles, Dimitri turned to Anya. "Come on," he said sadly. "It's time."

Arm in arm, Dimitri and Anya walked down the aisle and into the corridor.

Anya tried to stop shaking. In a few minutes it would be over. If the Empress believed her, voilà! A new home, a new family. Everything she'd always wanted.

Then why was she so afraid—and sad?

Dimitri was clutching her arm tightly. All the usual energy seemed to have drained from his face.

Maybe he was feeling the same way. After all they'd been through, had they grown fond of each other?

No, she realized, it was more than that. Much more. Dimitri was a part of who she was. A part of what she would always be. Anya loved him. And if she became the Princess, she would lose him.

Dimitri stopped in front of a wooden door, which led to the

Empress's private box. "Wait here just a minute. I'll go in and announce you properly."

He turned away, but Anya pulled him back. "Dimitri? Look, we've been through a lot together . . . and I just wanted to"—*What if he laughs at me?* she thought. *What if he hates me?*—"well, thank you," she blurted out. "Yes. Thank you for everything."

"Anya, I . . ." Dimitri began shyly.

Anya's pulse quickened. Could it be? Did he have feelings for her?

Dimitri's words caught in his throat for a moment. "I wanted to wish you good luck, I guess."

"Oh," Anya muttered.

Dimitri turned and stepped through the door. Anya waited a moment, then pressed her ear to it.

"Please inform Her Majesty, the Dowager Empress, that I have found her granddaughter," Dimitri announced. "She's waiting to see her just outside the door."

Empress Marie's reply was sharp. "You may tell that impertinent young man that I have seen enough Anastasias to last me a lifetime. Now, if you'll excuse me, I wish to live out the remainder of my lonely life in peace."

"Um, you'd better go," murmured Sophie's voice.

"Your Majesty," Dimitri pressed on, "my name is Dimitri. I used to work at the palace."

"Dimitri . . ." the Empress repeated. "I've heard of you. You're

that con man from St. Petersburg, who was holding auditions to find an Anastasia look-alike!"

Con man? Auditions? Look-alike? Anya was stunned. Was *this* what Dimitri was up to?

"But Your Grace," Dimitri's voice stammered, "it's not what you think. We've come all the way from Russia—"

"How much pain will you inflict on an old woman for money?" Empress Marie asked. "Guards, remove him at once!"

"But she *is* Anastasia!" Dimitri sputtered. "If you'll only speak to her—"

The door flew open and Dimitri tumbled out.

Anya did not help him up. She could barely speak. "It was all a lie, wasn't it? You *used* me! I was just a part of your con, to get her money!"

"No!" Dimitri shot back, scrambling to his feet. "It may have started out that way—but everything's different now, because you really are Anastasia. You *are!*"

"From the beginning you lied—and I not only believed you, I actually . . ." *Loved you,* she was going to say. But she was not going to give him the satisfaction of hearing it.

"Anya, please! When you spoke of the hidden door of the wall opening that time, and the little boy? Listen to me, that was—"

"No! You just leave me alone!"

Dimitri grabbed her arm. "Anya, please! You have to know the truth!"

The truth? What nerve to speak of truth!

Anya could not listen to any more. She had been fooled once too often.

Suddenly, she smacked him across the face.

Then she spun away, disappearing into the crowd before he could see her begin to cry.

chapter 12

Gone. She was gone.

Anya had completely misunderstood. And now she was walking away from everything—royalty, family, a life.

Dimitri searched frantically through the intermission crowd. Out of the corner of his eye, he spotted Empress Marie barreling through the crowd, still scowling.

At the curb, a chauffeur held a car door open for her.

This was his chance!

Dimitri ran to the sidewalk. He pushed the chauffeur aside and climbed into the driver's seat.

Screeeeee! The tires squealed as he raced away.

"Ilya!" Empress Marie called out. "Slow down!"

"I'm not Ilya," Dimitri replied, glancing over his shoulder, "and I won't slow down. Not until you listen."

In the rearview mirror, Dimitri could see the look of shock on Empress Marie's face. *"You!"* she gasped. "How dare you? *Stop this car immediately!"*

Dimitri pulled to a screeching halt in front of Sophie's mansion. He jumped out and ran to the Empress's window. "You have to believe her!" he pleaded, pulling the music box out of his backpack. "Do you recognize this?"

Empress Marie took the box and cradled it to her chest. Her voice was a choked whisper. "Where did you get this?"

"I know you've been hurt," Dimitri said gently. "But it's possible that she's been as lost and alone as you."

"You'll stop at nothing, will you?" Empress Marie cried, her eyes red and accusing.

Dimitri met her glance squarely. "I'm probably almost as stubborn as you are."

Inside Sophie's house, Anya threw her clothing into a suitcase. It was nice that Sophie had let her change there, after the shopping trip. But Anya did not feel like leaving a thank-you note. Maybe Sophie was in on the trick too. Maybe Dimitri the Sneak had promised to pay her.

At a sudden knock on the door, Anya tensed up. "Go away, Dimitri!" she called out.

But the door opened. And Empress Marie walked in.

"Oh!" Anya said. "I thought you were—"

"I know very well who you thought I was," the Empress replied coldly. "Who exactly are you?"

"I . . . I was hoping you'd tell me."

Empress Marie let out a weary sigh. "My dear, I'm old, and I'm tired of being conned and tricked."

"I don't want to trick you," Anya said.

"And I suppose the money doesn't interest you either?"

"I just want to know who I am, and whether or not I belong to a family—*your* family."

"You're a very good actress," the Empress said flatly. "The best yet, in fact. But I've had enough."

As the old woman turned to leave, Anya caught a whiff of something familiar. "Peppermint . . ." she said.

Empress Marie stopped. She faced Anya again, a suspicious look in her eye. "Yes. An oil for my hands."

"I spilled a bottle. . . ." Anya paused as the memory flowed into her mind. "The carpet was soaked, and it forever smelled of peppermint. Like you! I . . . I used to lie there on that rug—and oh, how I missed you when you went away, when you came here, to Paris."

The Empress's face was chalk-white. Anya began playing with the key around her neck.

"What is that?" Empress Marie asked.

"This?" Anya held up the key. "Well, I've always had it, ever since before I can remember."

The Empress reached into her evening bag and pulled out the music box. "It was our secret," she said, her eyes moistening. "My Anastasia's and mine."

"The music box . . . to sing me to sleep when you were in Paris . . ." Anya inserted the key into the box and turned.

A melody lilted out, soft and tinkly. Anya began humming along. She knew it well. Note for note.

Then came the words. Spilling lightly out of Anya's mouth, as if she'd sung them every day of her life.

She and Empress Marie looked at each other through eyes glazed with tears.

"Anastasia!" The Empress's voice cracked as she held out her arms. *"My Anastasia!"*

Chapter 13

For years, the Romanov family had had nothing to rejoice about. Today they were making up for lost time. The Princess was alive, and it was time to celebrate!

Sophie's house echoed with laughing voices. Servants bustled about, cleaning and decorating. Everyone in the neighborhood could hear the joyful sounds—from the cathedral bell ringers to the Parisian sewer rats.

Lurking among those rats, directly below the house, were Rasputin and Bartok.

"Bartok! Get me a comb; find some cologne! I want to look my best," cackled Rasputin. "We're going to a party. We'll let Grand Duchess Anastasia have her moment. And then we'll kill her at the height of her glory."

Dimitri was grim as he entered Empress Marie's study. "You sent for me, Your Grace?" he asked.

The Empress gestured toward an open valise, full of money. "Ten million rubles, as promised," she said. "With my gratitude."

"I accept your gratitude, Your Highness," Dimitri said. "But I don't want the money."

"What do you want, then?" the Empress asked.

Dimitri struggled not to blurt out the truth. What could he say? *I want to marry your granddaughter? I want to share my wretched life with the Princess?*

No. If there was one thing Dimitri had learned on the streets, it was to quit when you know you've lost. And what he was losing was more precious than money. "Unfortunately, I want nothing you can give," he said.

But the Empress didn't seem to hear the answer. Her eyes were narrowing. "Young man, where did you get that music box?" She stepped closer to Dimitri, looking him squarely in the eye. "*You* were the boy, weren't you? The servant boy who got us out? You saved her life and mine, then you restored her to me—yet you want no reward?"

"Not anymore."

"Why the change of mind?"

Dimitri met her glance. Mustering all his courage, he said the truest words he could. "It was more a change of heart."

With that, he bowed quickly and left.

Anastasia had been a princess for only a short time, but she loved it. Especially the jewel-studded crown she wore. As she toured through the Empress's house, an elderly butler accompanied her. Anastasia remembered him from the old days. Memories

were coming back to her every minute.

When she saw Dimitri walking down the stairs from Empress Marie's study, Anastasia stopped in her tracks. Why was the traitor still in the house? Was he planning to spoil her most glorious day?

"Hello, Dimitri," she said stiffly. "Did you collect your reward?"

"My business is complete," Dimitri mumbled.

"Young man," the butler scolded, "you will bow and address the Princess as 'Your Highness.'"

Dimitri bowed obediently. "I'm glad you found what you were looking for, Your Highness."

"Yes," Anastasia replied. "I'm glad you did too."

Dimitri bowed again and walked away.

Anastasia's anger began to fade. For someone who had just collected a reward, Dimitri had not seemed happy. Far from it. Miserable, perhaps. Completely heartbroken.

Anastasia swallowed hard. Dimitri had looked exactly the way she felt.

Later that day, Dimitri trudged into Empress Marie's apartment. There, Vladimir stood radiantly before a mirror, admiring his own fancy outfit. Pooka pranced at his feet, wearing a small crown and sword.

The Empress had agreed to let the two men use the apartment as a changing room for the party. But Dimitri had no intention of attending.

He picked up his backpack off the floor and slung it over his shoulder. "Well, Vlad, if you're ever in St. Petersburg again, look me up."

Vladimir embraced him. "You're making a mistake."

"Trust me, this is the one thing I'm doing right," Dimitri replied. He knelt down and scratched Pooka's nose. "So long, mutt."

Pooka whimpered softly. Vladimir looked on the verge of tears. But Dimitri had made up his mind.

He walked away without looking back.

Chapter 14

Anastasia . . . *she will rise again*.

The name—and its meaning—was on the lips of everyone in Europe. Only the elegant Grand Palais was large enough to hold an appropriate party. Royalty flocked to it from across the continent. The foyer was a sea of elegant people in elegant clothes, swaying to the music of a full orchestra.

Anastasia recognized many of the faces now. They belonged to her aunts and uncles and cousins who had escaped. But the one face she longed to see was not there.

She was startled by the voice of Empress Marie behind her. "He's not there," Marie said.

Anastasia tried to pretend she didn't know who her grandmother was talking about. "Who's not there, Grandmama?" she asked.

But Marie already knew her granddaughter too well. "A young man with a music box," she said, smiling.

Anastasia thought about Dimitri and the reward money. "It doesn't matter, Grandmama," she said quickly. "Finding you again,

finding what I could not even remember I had lost, that's what matters now."

Grandmother and granddaughter embraced, struggling to hold back bittersweet tears. But even as she clasped her long-lost granddaughter in her arms, Marie knew that Anastasia deserved to know the truth.

"He didn't take the money," Marie said.

Anastasia backed away. "He . . . didn't . . ." she stammered in confusion.

"He didn't take it," Marie repeated with a sad smile. "You will have to decide what to do, my darling. There is no place for him out there in that glittering crowd. But whatever you choose, I will hold you in my heart always."

Whatever I choose? What does she mean? If Dimitri didn't want the money, why did he go through with all of this?

Anastasia turned to Marie for guidance, but her grandmother had gone. The room was empty and still; the silence was broken only by the sounds of Pooka's barking outside. Listening intently, Anastasia turned toward the window. Pooka's barking came from beyond the terrace. Anastasia entered the dark garden to search for him.

At the train station, Dimitri edged forward in the ticket line. Soon he would be away from Paris. Soon he would start forgetting.

But the closer he was to the booth, the more he thought about

Anastasia. About how much he felt for her.

"Tell her!" cried a voice behind him.

Huh? Dimitri was jarred out of his daydream. He was first in line now. The ticket woman glared at him. "Where to, sir?"

"Come on, *tell her*!" urged the impatient traveler behind him.

"I will!" Dimitri grinned. "I'll tell her I love her!" He began to run.

Anastasia moved slowly through the dimly lit garden. "Pooka?" she called out. But Pooka's barking seemed to be coming from every direction at once, and she quickly lost her way. She heard him bark again and again, and she whirled toward the sound, gasping when she came face to face with a towering bush. It hadn't been there before!

"Pooka?" she called, her voice sounding more and more frightened. She turned away, only to be confronted with yet another bush that blocked her path. She was about to panic when Pooka dashed up to her. Together they pushed their way through a small opening in the bushes. Anastasia's happiness at finding Pooka quickly vanished as she heard someone or something saying her name.

"*An-a-sta-sia*," the creature moaned. Her eyes widened in fear. The creature's face looked horribly familiar, like a monster from a nightmare. But who was he?

"I'll give you a hint," he sneered. "You last saw me at a party

like this one. A party that was followed by a tragic night on the ice!"

He aimed his green, glowing reliquary at Anastasia. A stream of smoke billowed out of the reliquary. Anastasia was thrown to the ground. The blow jarred her memory.

"Rasputin!" she spat in disgust.

"Exactly!" he shrieked. "I was destroyed by your despicable family. But what goes around comes around!"

"I'm not afraid of you," Anastasia said calmly. Enraged, Rasputin blasted her over the side of the bridge with a stream of snow and ice.

"Say your prayers, Anastasia!" he cackled. "No one can save you!"

"Wanna bet?" Dimitri asked with a grin, as he rushed fearlessly toward Rasputin. Dimitri delivered a devastating punch to Rasputin's jaw.

"How enchanting. Together again. For the last time!" he laughed, blasting Dimitri with his reliquary. Chortling gleefully, Rasputin peered over the bridge toward the icy waters below. Anastasia and Pooka were nowhere to be seen. "Finally, the last Romanov death!" he cried. "Long live the Romanovs!"

"I couldn't have said it better myself," said Anastasia.

She lunged toward him and reached for the reliquary, but Rasputin shot a stream of minions back at her.

While Rasputin was distracted, Pooka leaped up, grabbed the reliquary in his mouth, and raced it over to Anastasia. The Princess

smiled in satisfaction, knowing she had at last defeated the evil Rasputin. But her smile faded when she caught a glimpse of Dimitri lying still just a few feet away.

"This is for Dimitri," she said, stomping on the reliquary. "This is for my family!" she added, stepping on it again. "And this is for you!" she shouted as the reliquary finally broke.

It exploded instantly, releasing an eerie green light and a whirlwind of minions that washed over Rasputin. Screaming, Rasputin glowed and then began to melt, leaving a rattling skeleton that crumbled into dust.

Anastasia hurried to Dimitri's side. She stroked his hair, and suddenly he groaned!

"Dimitri," she whispered, "you didn't take the money."

"I couldn't," he replied, and suddenly Anastasia understood. They embraced, but the romantic spell was broken by Pooka's barking. He returned the crown to Anastasia.

Both Pooka and Dimitri looked at Anastasia, wondering anxiously what she would do. Anastasia looked at Dimitri. At the crown. Then at Dimitri. And back at the crown.

Anastasia remembered the words Marie had spoken earlier that evening. "Whatever you choose, I will hold you in my heart always." So this was the choice her grandmother had been talking about.

A few hours later, the crown sat in lonely splendor on a table in the Grand Palais next to a note from Anastasia.

"It seems like only yesterday she came here!" said Sophie softly.

"At least we had that yesterday," Marie replied. "Now she has her tomorrow."

Dimitri and Anastasia stood together on the riverbank. Finally they kissed, and Pooka blushed. Anastasia knew she would never be alone again. They were the happiest people in Paris.

At that moment, their life together was beginning.

And that was enough.

A treasure of inspired filmmaking filled with humor and wonderful music! *Anastasia* is a spectacular, full-length animated feature film from master animators Don Bluth and Gary Goldman. The legend of the lost princess who is searching for her family is transcendent and moving, told with strong humor, sly wit, and dazzling animation. *Anastasia* captures the triumphant spirit of a young woman who loses everything in her life and fights to get it back. The first release from Fox Animation Studios, the most technically advanced facility of its kind, *Anastasia* will be released in fall 1997.

Drawing on the opulence of the Russian Empire, the glorious and gilded city of St. Petersburg, and the magnificence of 1920s Paris, *Anastasia* captures the visual splendor of the periods. A deftly written script complements characters beautifully drawn and painstakingly brought to life. The story overflows with adventure and romance, and is moved along by a sparkling, new song score by successful Broadway collaborators Lynn Ahrens and Stephen Flaherty.

Superstar Meg Ryan stars as the voice of the lost princess, who we encounter first as an orphan named Anya. Driven to find her true identity and begin a new life, Anya fights against all obstacles, natural and supernatural. John Cusack takes on the

role of Dimitri, the handsome, slick con artist who convinces the orphan Anya to travel with him to Paris and impersonate Anastasia—not realizing she actually is the Princess. Beloved actress Angela Lansbury is the voice of the Grand Duchess Marie, Anastasia's grandmother, whose broken heart is mended when she is at long last reunited with her adored granddaughter.

Brilliant comic actor Christopher Lloyd is the evil sorcerer Rasputin, who vows his revenge when he is banished from the Romanov court. Hank Azaria is Bartok, an albino bat and Rasputin's wisecracking sidekick. Broadway's Bernadette Peters plays Marie's scatterbrained lady-in-waiting, Sophie, to Kelsey Grammer's Vladimir, a faded, romantic aristocrat who is Dimitri's consort. Rounding out this exciting ensemble of Hollywood stars is talented actress Kirsten Dunst as the voice of the young Princess Anastasia.

The elements of *Anastasia* are those of Hollywood's greatest successes—spirited comedy, riveting adventure, soaring musical numbers, haunting melodies, and spectacular animation. Destined to become a family classic, audiences of all ages will cherish the adventure and romance of *Anastasia.*